D0574718

Max and the Mail

The Sound of M

by Joanne Meier and Cecilia Minden • illustrated by Bob Ostrom

The
Child's
World®

Published by The Child's World®
1980 Lookout Drive
Mankato, MN 56003-1705
800-599-READ
www.childsworld.com

The Child's World®: Mary Berendes, Publishing Director
The Design Lab: Design and page production

Library of Congress Cataloging-in-Publication Data
Meier, Joanne D.
  Max and the mail : the sound of m / by Joanne Meier
and Cecilia Minden ; illustrated by Bob Ostrom.
    p. cm.
  ISBN 978-1-60253-409-4 (library bound : alk. paper)
  1. English language—Consonants—Juvenile literature.
  2. English language—Phonetics—Juvenile literature 3.
Reading—Phonetic method—Juvenile literature. I. Minden,
Cecilia. II. Ostrom, Bob. III. Title.
  PE1159.M46 2010
  [E]—dc22   2010002922

Printed in the United States of America in Mankato, MN.
July 2010
F11538

NOTE TO PARENTS AND EDUCATORS:

The Child's World® has created this series with the
goal of exposing children to engaging stories and
illustrations that assist in phonics development.
The books in the series will help children learn the
relationships between the letters of written language
and the individual sounds of spoken language. This
contact helps children learn to use these relationships
to read and write words.

The books in this series follow a similar format. An
introductory page, to be read by an adult, introduces
the child to the phonics feature, or sound, that will be
highlighted in the book. Read this page to the child,
stressing the phonic feature. Help the student learn
how to form the sound with her mouth. The story and
engaging illustrations follow the introduction. At the
end of the story, word lists categorize the feature
words into their phonic elements.

Each book in this series has been carefully written
to meet specific readability requirements. Close
attention has been paid to elements such as word
count, sentence length, and vocabulary. Readability
formulas measure the ease with which the text can
be read and understood. Each book in this series has
been analyzed using the Spache readability formula.

Reading research suggests that systematic phonics
instruction can greatly improve students' word recog-
nition, spelling, and comprehension skills. This series
assists in the teaching of phonics by providing students
with important opportunities to apply their knowledge
of phonics as they read words, sentences, and text.

This is the letter m.

In this book, you will read words that have the **m** sound as in: *mail, milk, mother,* and *man.*

Today is a big day for Max.

He might get some mail.

Max makes his bed.
He puts most of his
toys away.

Max makes his breakfast.

He likes toast and milk.

After breakfast, Max gets dressed. He can do most of it by himself. His mother helps with the rest.

Max and his mother get the mail. Most of it is for Max's mother.

Some mail is for Max!

It is a new book.

That makes Max happy.

"May I read it now?"
asks Max.

"Yes, you may," says Mother.
"Let's read it together."

Max and his mother read the book. It is about a man who walked on the moon.

"One day I will walk on the moon," says Max. Would you like to walk on the moon like Max?

Fun Facts

Do you think you might want to visit the moon? You'll probably find it very different from life on Earth. There is no water on the surface of the moon, and there aren't any clouds. Instead of earthquakes, the moon has what are called "moonquakes." Also, time passes more slowly on the moon than it does on Earth. One day on the moon is 655 hours long!

Suppose you live in Missouri and need to mail a letter to a friend in California. You know that your friend will receive his letter in the mail about two to three days after you send it. In the 1800s, however, it would probably have taken about 10 days for the letter to reach your friend. Employees of a mail service called the Pony Express rode on horseback between Missouri and California and delivered letters and packages along the way.

Activity

Studying the Moon

On a clear night, you can see the moon in the sky. If you want a closer view, ask your parents if they have a *telescope*. A telescope is a device that makes faraway objects appear to be closer. With the help of a telescope, you will be able to see the surface of the moon more clearly. You might also be able to see several stars and possibly even some planets!

To Learn More

Books
About the Sound of M
Moncure, Jane Belk. *My "m" Sound Box®*. Mankato, MN: The Child's World, 2009.

About Mail
Gibbons, Gail. *The Post Office Book: Mail and How It Moves*. New York: Harper & Row, 1986.
Thaler, Mike, and Jerry Smath (illustrator). *Never Mail an Elephant*. Mahwah, NJ: Troll, 1994.

About the Moon
Gibbons, Gail. *The Moon Book*. New York: Holiday House, 1997.
Rylant, Cynthia, and Mark Siegel (illustrator). *Long Night Moon*. New York: Simon & Schuster Books for Young Readers, 2004.

About Mothers
Lasky, Kathryn, and LeUyen Pham (illustrator). *Before I Was Your Mother*. San Diego: Harcourt, 2003.
Ryder, Joanne, and Peter Catalanotto (illustrator). *My Mother's Voice*. New York: HarperCollins, 2006.

Web Sites
Visit our home page for lots of links about the Sound of M:
childsworld.com/links

Note to Parents, Teachers, and Librarians: We routinely check our Web links to make sure they're safe, active sites—so encourage your readers to check them out!

M Feature Words

Proper Names
Max

Feature Words in Initial Position
made

mail

make

man

may

might

milk

moon

most

mother

Feature Word in Medial Position
himself

About the Authors

Joanne Meier, PhD, has worked as an elementary school teacher, university professor, and researcher. She earned her BA in early childhood education from the University of South Carolina, and her MEd and PhD in education from the University of Virginia. She currently works as a literacy consultant for schools and private organizations. Joanne lives in Virginia with her husband Eric, daughters Kella and Erin, two cats, and a gerbil.

Cecilia Minden, PhD, is the former director of the Language and Literacy Program at the Harvard Graduate School of Education. She is now a reading consultant for school and library publications. She earned her PhD in reading education from the University of Virginia. Cecilia and her husband, Dave Cupp, live outside Chapel Hill, North Carolina. They enjoy sharing their love of reading with their grandchildren, Chelsea and Qadir.

About the Illustrator

Bob Ostrom has been illustrating children's books for nearly twenty years. A graduate of the New England School of Art & Design at Suffolk University, Bob has worked for such companies as Disney, Nickelodeon, and Cartoon Network. He lives in North Carolina with his wife Melissa and three children, Will, Charlie, and Mae.